DATE DUE

FE 10 '10		
FE 22 '10		
JY 7 '10		
JY 26 '10		
OC 25 '11		
OC 3 0 '__		
DE 0 8 '__		
FE 0 __ '__		
MY 2 5 '__		

With love for my parents, Peter and Verna Coleman —U.D.

For Beck, William, and Charlotte —A.J.

Text copyright © 2009 by Ursula Dubosarsky
Pictures copyright © 2009 by Andrew Joyner
All rights reserved
First published in Australia by Penguin Books for Children, 2009
Printed in October 2009 in China by South China Printing Co. Ltd.,
Dongguan City, Guangdong Province
First American edition, 2009
3 5 7 9 10 8 6 4 2

www.fsgkidsbooks.com

Library of Congress Cataloging-in-Publication Data
Dubosarsky, Ursula, date.
    The terrible plop / Ursula Dubosarsky ; pictures by Andrew Joyner.— 1st American ed.
        p.   cm.
    Summary: When a mysterious sound sends the whole forest running away in fear, only the
littlest rabbit is courageous enough to discover what really happened.
    ISBN: 978-0-374-37428-0
    [1. Stories in rhyme.   2. Rabbits—Fiction.   3. Forest animals—Fiction.   4. Fear—Fiction.
5. Courage—Fiction.]   I. Joyner, Andrew, ill.   II. Title.

PZ8.3.D8517 Te 2009
[E]—dc22

                                                                                                    2008043323

The TERRIBLE PLOP

Ursula Dubosarsky

Pictures by Andrew Joyner

Farrar, Straus and Giroux / New York

Six little rabbits
Down by the lake
Munching on carrots
And chocolate cake.

Next to the lake
In a tree up high
A round red apple
Swings in the sky.

Soft is the wind
And the tree bends low.
The round red apple
Is all aglow.

Up jump the rabbits—
Hop hop hop!

They shout to each other,
"Run! Don't stop!
We must get away
From the Terrible PLOP!"

"Wait, little rabbits,"
Calls the fox as they pass.
"Where are you hopping to
So very fast?"

But the rabbits cry back,
"We cannot stop!
We must get away
From the Terrible PLOP!"

The Terrible PLOP?
Thinks the fox in fear.
Maybe I'd better
Get out of here!

"Goodbye, friend monkey,
I cannot stop.
I must get away
From the Terrible PLOP!"

He runs with the rabbits,
The monkey and the cat,

The pig and the elephant,

The tiger and the bat.

Soon all the animals,
One by one,
Out of the forest
They come at a run.

Out comes the leopard!
Out comes the goose!
Out comes the antelope!
Out comes the moose!

They do not stay.
They do not stop.
They run run run
From the Terrible PLOP.

At last they come
To the big brown bear
Sunning himself
In a folding chair.

"What's this?" says the big brown bear
   With a frown.
"Where are you running to?
   Stop! Slow down!"

"No, no, brown bear,
We cannot stop.
We must get away
From the Terrible PLOP!"

"The Terrible PLOP?
What do I care
About a silly old PLOP?"
Yawns the big brown bear.

"Oh no, brown bear," they cry.
"You're wrong!
The PLOP is fierce!
The PLOP is strong!
It's coming to get us,
It's coming, you'll see!"

"WHAT?"
growls the brown bear,
"Stronger than

ME?"

And he grabs with his paw
At the one coming last—
The littlest rabbit
Who's not very fast.

The littlest rabbit
With the littlest hop
But the greatest fear
Of the Terrible PLOP.

"Now, little rabbit,
You show me where
Is the place of the PLOP,"
Snarls the big brown bear.

"Oh please, big bear,
Don't make me go.
I'm very afraid
Of the PLOP, you know!"

"Afraid of the PLOP?
You show me where

OR I'LL EAT YOU UP!"

Roars the big brown bear.

Poor little rabbit.
Blink blink blink.
Poor little rabbit.
Think think think.

"I'm afraid of the PLOP.
I'm afraid of the bear.
But the bear is here
And the PLOP is there!"

Brave little rabbit,
Hop hop hop.
Back to the lake
And the Terrible PLOP.

Big brown bear
Slowly comes to a stop.
"So where," says the bear,
"Is this Terrible PLOP?"

The sun is soft,
The water is still.
An evening wind
Rolls down from the hill.

Tall and dark
Stands the big brown bear,
Dark and strong
With his nose in the air.

Next to the lake
In a tree up high
A round red apple
Swings in the sky.

Suddenly comes
A terrible

PLOP!

But this time the rabbit
Does not hop.

The wind rolls down
From the top of the hill,
But this time the littlest rabbit
Sits still,

And turns to speak
To the big brown bear.
But the big brown bear . . .

The rabbit calls out
To the big brown bear,
"Where are you going to,
Bear, oh where?"
The bear cries back,

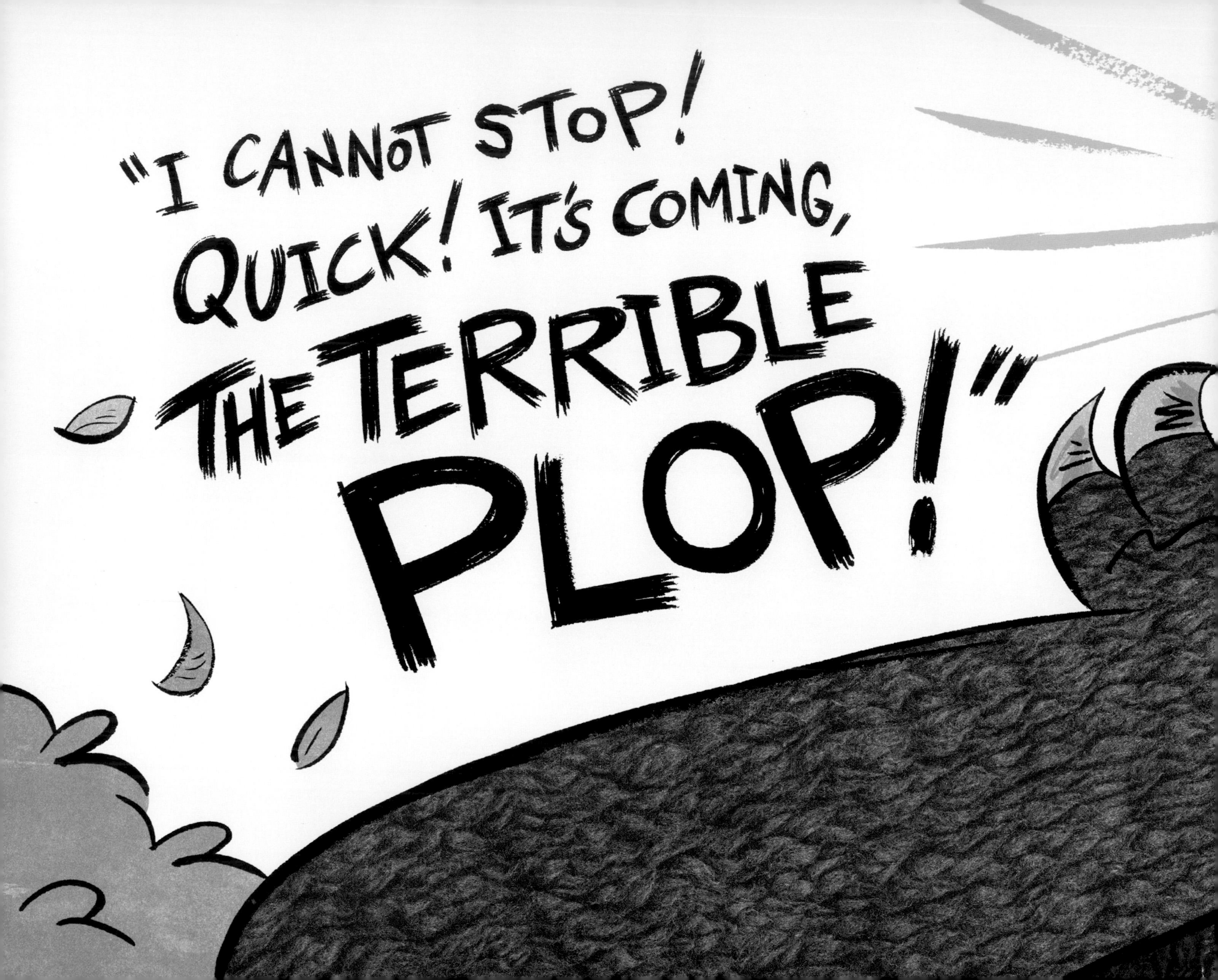
"I CANNOT STOP!
QUICK! IT'S COMING,
THE TERRIBLE
PLOP!"

One little rabbit
Down by the lake
Happily munching on
Chocolate cake.

"All this running
Should really stop . . .

Who's afraid
Of a silly old PLOP?"